Jade McKade

Written by Jane Carroll
Illustrated by Virginia Barrett

An easy-to-read SOLO
for beginning readers

SOLOS

Southwood Books Limited
4 Southwood Lawn Road
London N6 5SF

First published in Australia by Omnibus Books 1997

This edition published in the UK under licence from
Omnibus Books by
Southwood Books Limited, 2000

Text copyright © Jane Carroll 1997
Illustrations copyright © Virginia Barrett 1997

Cover design by Lyn Mitchell

ISBN 1 903207 16 9

Printed in Hong Kong

A CIP catalogue record for this book is available
from the British Library

For Jeanie, who didn't want to go

to school – J.C.

For Katy – V.B.

Chapter 1

Jade McKade loved to climb the tree in her back garden. She loved to race her go-cart down the hill.

She loved to play monsters and dragons with the kids next door.

But Jade McKade didn't love going to school.

Every morning at breakfast time she said, "I don't want to go to school."

All the way to the bus stop she shouted, "I don't want to go to school!"

In the bus she wrote with her finger on the window, *I don't want to go to school.*

Chapter 2

One morning Jade wouldn't get out of bed.

"It's time you got dressed," said Mum.

"You'll be late for school," said Dad.

"And you'll make me late too!"
yelled Jemma, her big sister.

"Go away and leave me alone"
said Jade from under her duvet.

Jade took so long to get out
of bed, she and Jemma missed the
bus. Mum said, "I'll have to drive
you. I'll be late for work. Get into
the car. Hurry up!"

"But I haven't had breakfast!" said Jade.

"Bring it with you," said Mum.

"But I'm still in my pyjamas!" wailed Jade.

"Then you can go to school in your pyjamas!" said Mum. "Jade McKade, we are going to school, and we are going *now*."

Jade had to get dressed in the
car. All the way she shouted, "I don't
want to go to school! I don't want to
go to school!"

Mum took Jade and Jemma into
the playground. The other kids were
lining up to go in to class.

"You're late," said Mum. "Hurry up. Off you go."

Chapter 3

At lunch time a man came with a camera to take the children's photos.

The boys and girls in Jade's class did their hair. They brushed the crumbs off their jumpers.

They lined up in rows with the tallest at the back and the smallest at the front. They held their hands behind their backs.

"Big smile!" said the man with the camera.

Jade pulled a face.

"We'll try that again," said the man. "All together, say *cheese*."

"Cheeeeeeeese!" said the children.

"Bum," said Jade, and folded her arms.

"Little girl in the front row," said the man. "You're spoiling the photo."

"Jade McKade, where's your happy smile?" said the teacher.

"Jade McKade, you're terrible," whispered her friend, Gabby Green. She smiled at Jade and Jade smiled back.

Chapter 4

The next morning Mum said, "Time to get up, Jade."

Dad said, "Hurry up and get dressed, Jade."

Jemma said, "If you make me late for school today, I'll turn you into a fly and squash you!"

Jade pulled the duvet up to her
chin and said, "I feel sick."

"Don't be silly," said Mum.

"Don't pretend," said Dad.

"Do you want me to squash you now?" yelled Jemma.

"But I've got spots," wailed Jade. "I *am* sick."

And she was..

Chapter 5

Jade had spots on her face and spots on her tummy. She had spots in her ears and spots in her throat.

She had spots between her toes and spots up her nose.

She wasn't allowed to go to school. She had to stay home in bed.

That afternoon Jemma came home from school and counted the spots on Jade's tummy.

"Four hundred and six," she said. "Today Gabby Green brought a birthday cake to school. She kept a piece and asked me to bring it home for you. But I knew you were sick, so I ate it."

"See if I care," said Jade.

Chapter 6

The next afternoon Jemma counted the spots on Jade's back. "Three hundred and seventy-seven," she said. "Today was Games Day. We had sack races and egg-and-spoon races. We had a Bouncy Castle too."

"So what," said Jade.

The next afternoon Jemma counted the spots between Jade's toes.

"Sixty-three," she said. "Tomorrow
all the kids from school are going
to the Show."

"Can I come too?" said Jade.

"You have to stay in bed," said Jemma. "You're not allowed to go."

Chapter 7

The next afternoon Jemma checked the spots in Jade's throat and the spots in her ears.

She said, "The Show was cool fun. I had a hot dog and chips and candy floss.

"Then I went on the swings and I wasn't even sick. Gabby Green said she wished you were there."

Jade didn't say anything. A big
tear sneaked down her cheek.

That night, when Mum came to kiss her goodnight, Jade said, "Mum, when can I go back to school?"

"As soon as the spots have gone and you feel better," said Mum. She looked at Jade's tummy. "Lots of spots have gone already. You'll be better soon." She gave Jade a hug and kissed her goodnight.

Chapter 8

When the spots had all gone and Jade felt better, Mum drove her to school.

Jade and Jemma walked in to the playground together. The kids in Jade's class ran up to say hullo.

Gabby Green said, "You can sit next to me at lunch time." Then she said, "Guess what? We're having a fairy tale fancy dress parade. I'm the princess."

"What am I?" said Jade.

"You're the dragon," said Gabby.

"That's good," said Jade. "I like being a dragon."

Chapter 9

All the mums and dads came to see the parade. They clapped and cheered.

Jade's mum and dad clapped the loudest for the dragon.

After the parade the teacher took a photo of the children in their costumes. "Look this way," he said. "Say *cheese!*"

"*Cheeeeeeeese!*" said the king, the queen, the princess, the witch and all the elves and fairies.

"Bum," said the dragon, and giggled.

Jane Carroll

When my mum was a little girl she didn't want to go to school. She walked along the brick wall outside her house singing, "I don't want to go to school, I don't want to go to school."

One day she got very sick. She had to stay home in bed for weeks. After a while she got bored with being at home. She wanted to go back to school! She kept singing, "I *want* to go to school, I *want* to go to school."

When my mum told me this I laughed. That's why I wrote the story about Jade McKade.

Virginia Barrett

Before I could draw the pictures for this book, I needed a model. I had to find a little girl who looked the way I thought Jade McKade did. I knew someone called Tina who had four daughters. If none of them was right, maybe Tina knew other little girls I could draw. I went to see her. The door was opened by my perfect Jade! There she was, with her hair all over the place, wearing jeans, and with a wicked smile. How lucky!

Thanks Katy, and thanks Tina!

More Solos!

Dog Star
Janeen Brian and Ann James

The Best Pet
Penny Matthews and Beth Norling

Fuzz the Famous Fly
Emily Rodda and Tom Jellett

Cat Chocolate
Kate Darling and Mitch Kane

Jade McKade
Jane Carroll and Virginia Barrett

I Want Earrings
Dyan Blacklock and Craig Smith

What a Mess Fang Fang
Sally Rippin

Cocky Colin
Richard Tulloch and Stephen Axelsen